Nobody Likes My Spider

Bill Gillham

Illustrated by Margaret Chamberlain

Methuen Children's Books

Nobody likes my spider.

Except me!

My Mum doesn't like him.

Nor does our cat.

But my spider is friendly.

He likes to play.

And share your food.

He goes with you everywhere.

Everywhere!

But people are mean to him.

They swat him . . .

and spray him . . .

and throw things at him.

But he always pops up again

when you don't expect it!

One day we had a big surprise.

He brought a wife . . .

and six little children.

"Get them out of here!"
shouted Mum.

So I took them
up to my bedroom.

Because nobody likes
my spiders.

Except me!

How to pair read

1 Sit the child next to you, so that you can both see the book.

2 Tell the child you are *both* going to read the story *at the same time.* To begin with the child will be hesitant: adjust your speed so that you are reading almost simultaneously, *pointing to the words* as you go.

3 If the child makes a mistake, repeat the correct word but *keep going* so that fluency is maintained.

4 Gradually increase your speed once you and the child are reading together.

5 As the child becomes more confident, lower your voice and, progressively, try dropping out altogether.

6 If the child stumbles or gets stuck, give the correct word and continue 'pair-reading' to support fluency, dropping out again quite quickly.

7 Read the story *right through* once a day but not more than twice, so that it stays fresh.

8 After about 5–8 readings the child will usually be reading the book independently.

In its original form paired reading was first devised by Roger Morgan and Elizabeth Lyon, and described in a paper published in the Journal of Child Psychology and Psychiatry (1979).

First published in Great Britain in 1986
by Methuen Children's Books Ltd, 11 New Fetter Lane, London EC4P 4EE
Text copyright © 1986 Bill Gillham. Illustrations copyright © 1986 Margaret Chamberlain
Printed in Great Britain ISBN 0 416 95820 6